The Spy Code Caper

by Susan Pearson

illustrated by
Gioia Fiammenghi

SIMON & SCHUSTER BOOKS FOR YOUNG READERS
PUBLISHED BY SIMON & SCHUSTER
New York • London • Toronto • Sydney • Tokyo • Singapore

For Juren, with tons of hugs — SP

To my family — GF

 SIMON & SCHUSTER BOOKS FOR YOUNG READERS
Simon & Schuster Building, Rockefeller Center, 1230 Avenue of the Americas, New York,
New York 10020. Text copyright © 1991 by Susan Pearson. Illustrations copyright © 1991
by Gioia Fiammenghi. All rights reserved including the right of reproduction in whole or
in part in any form. SIMON & SCHUSTER BOOKS FOR YOUNG READERS is a trademark of
Simon & Schuster.
Designed by Lucille Chomowicz
Manufactured in the United States of America.
10 9 8 7 6 5 4 3 2 1   (pbk) 10 9 8 7 6 5 4 3 2 1
Library of Congress Cataloging-in-Publication Data: Pearson, Susan. The spy caper / by
Susan Pearson; illustrated by Gioia Fiammenghi. Summary: Ernie uses her eagle eye to solve
the mystery of the Maple Street spy ring. [1. Mystery and detective stories.] I.
Fiammenghi, Gioia, ill. II. Title.
PZ7.P323316Ear 1991   [Fic]—dc20   91-15403 CIP
ISBN: 0-671-74071-7   ISBN: 0-671-74072-5 (pbk)

The Spy Code Caper

CONTENTS

CHAPTER 1

The Spy Across the Street

It was Thursday afternoon, and it was raining. Again. It had rained on Monday. It had rained on Tuesday. It had rained on Wednesday, too.

"What a dumb way to start our summer vacation," said Ernie. She was sitting on her front porch with the rest of the Martian Club. "I am bored already."

"Me, too," said R.T. She twisted one of her braids around her finger. Then she began to chew on it.

"Me, three," said William. He threw his crayon on the floor. "I have drawn one hundred and thirty-nine pictures this week."

1

Michael pulled off his headphones. He always wore an old set of headphones. That was how he listened to Mission Control. "What we need is a mystery," he said. "Then we would have something to do. And I bet you could find us one, Ernie. Just look around with your eagle eye."

It was true that Ernie had an eagle eye. Whenever Daddy lost his glasses, it was always Ernie who found them. Whenever Mommy lost an earring, Ernie found that, too. She had even solved some real mysteries.

"My eagle eye is for *solving* mysteries," said Ernie, "not for finding them."

"I'll find one, then," said Michael.

"I'll help," said R.T. "I am bored with being bored."

"Maybe one will walk right down the street," said William. "You never know with mysteries."

"Good thinking," said R.T. "Then we won't have to get wet looking for it."

"Let's get started," said Michael.

Ernie didn't think a mystery was about to happen on her street. But William was right—you never knew with mysteries. Maybe one could happen. Besides, they had already played every game in her game box at least ten times.

Ernie peered up the street. No mystery there, just houses and trees and bushes and rain. She peered down the street. More of the same.

Then a lady came around the corner. She held an umbrella in one hand. She held a leash in the other. At the end of the leash was a very wet dog. No mystery there, either.

It looked to Ernie as if mystery-finding was going to get boring in a hurry. She leaned back against the house. She shut her eyes. Maybe she would just dream about a mystery instead.

Plop-plop-plop-plop. The rain splashed on the porch roof. *Swish-sh-sh-sh*. A car drove through a puddle. *Click-click*. The car door opened. *Sla-a-a-m*. The car door shut.

"There it is," whispered Michael.

Ernie opened her eyes. "There what is?" she asked.

"Our mystery."

Sure enough, a mysterious-looking black car had stopped in front of the house across the street. A man had gotten out of it. He wore a black raincoat and black rubber boots and a black hat. The hat was pulled down over his forehead. Beneath the brim, Ernie could barely see his dark sunglasses.

"It's a spy," Michael said softly. "Wow!"

The man walked up the path to the front door. He climbed the steps to the porch. But he did not ring the doorbell. He did not knock on the door. He just reached for the doorknob. The door did not open. It was locked, and the man did not have a key.

"Who lives there?" whispered R.T.

"Nobody," Ernie whispered back. "The McGowans used to. They moved to California as soon as school was over."

"Then who is *that*?" whispered William. Ernie was wondering the same thing.

"I told you," Michael said. "It's a spy! Everyone knows that that is what spies wear—raincoats and sunglasses."

"Detectives dress that way, too," said William. "It could be a detective."

Ernie wasn't so sure. What would a detective or a spy be doing on *her* street? "It could just be the person who bought the McGowans' house," she said.

"Nah," said R.T. "That person would have a key."

"He has to be a spy," said Michael. "The sunglasses prove it. Who else would wear sunglasses on a rainy day?"

The man came down off the porch. He had pushed back his hat so Ernie could see his face a little better now. Stringy wet hair fell onto his face. His sunglasses were big and black. He walked to the living room window and peered in. Then he walked to the next window and peered in. Then he walked around the corner and disappeared into the backyard.

"We should follow him," said Michael.

"It's not raining so hard now."

"I'm not following any spy," said William.

"Me, neither!" said R.T.

"I'm not going alone," said Michael.

"You don't have to," Ernie said. "There he is again."

The strange man came around the other side of the house. He cut across the lawn. He opened the car door. He climbed in. As he shut the door, a piece of paper fluttered to the ground beside the car. Then the car drove away.

"Did you see that?" said R.T.

"I bet it's a spy message," said William.

"Come on!" shouted Michael. "We have to get it before it turns to mush in the rain."

The four friends tore off the porch. They ran to the curb. They looked up and down the street. No cars, no people, no anything. They raced across. Michael grabbed the piece of paper. Then they all ran back to Ernie's porch.

"What is it?" asked R.T. She was chewing on her braid again.

"Open it!" shouted William. "Quick!" He hopped from one foot to the other.

Ernie held her breath. Michael unfolded the piece of paper. He stared at the message written on it. R.T. and William and Ernie stared, too. William stopped hopping. R.T.'s braid dropped out of her open mouth. Ernie's tummy flip-flopped. The message was written in *code*!

CHAPTER 2

A New Case for Eagle Eye

It was still raining on Friday morning, but Ernie didn't care. She had a mystery to solve!

Ernie skipped into the kitchen. "I need a brain-food breakfast," she announced.

Mommy looked up over her newspaper and smiled. "Good morning, lamb," she said. "There are some bananas in the fruit bowl."

Ernie sliced a banana into a bowl. She thought for a second. Then she sliced another. Bananas were good brain food. She sat down at the kitchen table.

"Care for some cereal with your brain food?" Daddy asked. He passed her the box.

Ernie poured cereal over her bananas.

"Do we have any raisins?" she asked. "Raisins are good brain food, too."

"In the cupboard," said Mommy.

Ernie got a box of raisins. She poured some raisins over the cereal. Then she poured milk over everything.

Daddy looked over his paper at Mommy. "Looks like our eagle eye has a new case," he said.

"Mmm," said Mommy. "Must be a tough one to need all that brain food."

"The toughest," said Ernie. "Uncoding codes is the hardest work of all."

"Speaking of work," said Daddy, "I had better get a move on." He laid his newspaper on the table, picked up his briefcase, and kissed Ernie on top of her head. "Good luck, champ," he said.

Ernie just nodded. Her mouth was too full of brain food for her to speak.

Ernie skipped down the street through the rain. She sang a little brain-food song as she skipped.

"Brain food, brain food,
That's the food for me.
Goodness how delicious
Brainy food can be."

She cut through Michael's side yard. The Martian clubhouse was in his backyard. A sign on the door said:

MARTIAN CLUB
PRIVATE!
MARTIANS ONLY!
THIS MEANS
PRINCE MICHAEL
QUEEN ERNIE
KING WILLIAM
QUEEN R.T.
EVERYONE ELSE KEEP OUT!

Another sign said:

STAR FINDER
Travel through Space
with Commander Michael

When it wasn't the Martian clubhouse, the playhouse was Michael's spaceship.

The other Martians were already there. They were sitting on orange crates. R.T. and William were putting together a puzzle. Michael was mapping a journey through space.

William jumped up off his crate. He grinned at Ernie. "We waited for you," he said. "This code needs your eagle eye."

"Now we can get started," R.T. said. "Did you eat lots of brain food this morning, Ernie?"

Ernie nodded. She pulled up an orange crate. Michael pulled the coded message from his pocket. He set it on the floor where everyone could see it. It was a little wrinkled, but they could still read it.

1 = DR	6 = KI
2 = LL	7 = LR
3 = BA	8 = NG
4 = FA	9 = MAB
5 = EA	

"*Hmmm,*" said Ernie.

"*Hmmm,*" said Michael.

"*Hmmm,*" said R.T.

"What do you think it could mean?" asked William.

"Nothing good," said Michael. "I bet those numbers are spy targets. Number one is probably the mayor."

"Or a scientist," said R.T.

Ernie scratched her head. "I don't think the numbers stand for people," she said. "It looks more like the *letters* stand for people. They look like initials. DR could stand for David Ross."

"Who is David Ross?" asked R.T.

Ernie shrugged. "I don't know. I just made it up."

"A telephone book!" William shouted. "A telephone book would tell us all the DRs who live in White Bear Lake!"

Michael ran into his house. He came back with a telephone book.

Ernie opened it to the Rs. She ran her finger down the first column. "Here is a Daniel

Rabara," she said. "And here is a Donald Rabb." Ernie giggled. "There's a Peter Rabbit, too."

"It must be a store or something," said Michael. "Keep going."

There were three D. Rabins, and a Dirk and a Douglas Ralph. Three Ramseths— Darlene, Dwayne, and Dorothy. But the Ramseys were the worst yet. Two D. Ramseys, plus one David, one Deborah, one Delmar, one Dennis, and one Donna.

Ernie shut the book. "We'll never figure it out this way."

"Wait a minute," said Michael. "If the letters are initials, then the numbers could be just numbers. Target Number One is this DR person. The spy is hanging around the McGowans' house. So DR must live in this neighborhood. Right?"

"That makes sense," said R.T. "Do any of those DRs live on Maple Street, Ernie?"

Ernie opened the telephone book again. She ran her finger down the column of DRs.

"Nope," she said. "None on Maple Street. Besides, a spy ought to know his targets. He wouldn't have to make a list of them. I think this code is simpler than that."

"Well, then, what *is* it?" asked William.

Ernie shook her head. "I don't know yet," she said. "I need to think about it."

Ernie stood up. She stretched. Stretching sometimes helped her think. She walked to one end of the clubhouse. Then she walked to the other end. Walking sometimes helped her think, too. "Come on, brain food," she muttered. "Get busy."

Back and forth, back and forth she walked. This code was simple, she was sure of it. 1 = DR, 2 = LL, 3 = BA.

Suddenly, she had it! "This is not a code at all!" she cried. "It is the *de*coder!"

"Huh?" said Michael.

"What do you mean?" asked R.T.

"Tell us, Ernie," William said.

"Look," said Ernie. "The *real* codes are written in numbers. The numbers stand for these letters. If you have the decoder, you can read the messages!"

"Wow," said Michael. "And we have the decoder!"

"That sounds good," said R.T. "I think you are right, Ernie."

"Hooray for Eagle-Eye Ernie!" shouted William.

"Hooray for brain food!" Ernie shouted back. "Those bananas do it every time!"

CHAPTER 3

The Spy Ring

"Look," said R.T. "It stopped raining. The sun is out."

"When did that happen?" asked Ernie.

"While you were thinking," William told her.

"And now I am thinking," said Michael. "I am thinking that we should not be here. We should be on your front porch, Ernie, spying on the spy."

"I hope we didn't miss anything," said R.T. "I hope that spy stayed home this morning."

The Martians dashed out of the club-house. They raced down the street. They got

18

to Ernie's in the nick of time. A delivery truck was just pulling up in front of the McGowans' house.

Two men got out of the truck. They opened its back door. They began to carry boxes up onto the porch. Then one man shut the truck. The other pulled a key from his pocket. He unlocked the McGowans' front door. They carried all the boxes inside. Then they went inside, too. They shut the door behind them.

"How come *they* have a key?"

"Where is the spy?"

"What was in all those boxes?"

"What are the men doing in there?"

The Martians had a lot of questions. They didn't have any answers.

"We will have to wait and see, I guess," said R.T. "They won't be in there long."

But they were. Ten minutes passed. Then fifteen. Then twenty.

Ernie was puzzled. "What can they be doing?" she wondered. "Deliverymen don't stay in houses. They just deliver and go."

"These deliverymen are not deliverymen," said Michael. His voice was low and spooky. "They are part of the spy ring."

William shivered. "Can you see anything through the windows?"

"Not from here," said R.T.

"But we could from over there," said Ernie.

"I am not moving off this porch, Ernie," said William.

"We can't just walk over there and stare through the windows," said R.T.

"I know that," said Ernie. "But I have a plan. Wait here."

Ernie ran inside her house. She got a ball from her closet. Then she raced back to the porch. "Follow me," she told the Martians. She led them into her yard. "We are going to play catch." R.T. and Michael and William looked at Ernie with questions on their faces. Ernie grinned. "It's simple," she told them. "We are going to play miss-the-ball. You three will stand here. When I throw the ball to you, you will miss it. The ball will fly right past you. It will fly across the street into the McGowans' yard. Then we will have to go over there to get it. Got it?"

"I'm not going," said William.

"You don't have to," said Michael. "I will go."

"Me too," said R.T.

Michael and R.T. and William lined up. Ernie threw the ball to them. William caught it.

"Don't catch it, William," Ernie reminded him.

William tossed the ball back. Ernie threw it again. William caught it again.

"Cut that out, William!" said Michael.

"I don't think we should be doing this," said William.

"Come over here and be a thrower, then," said Ernie.

William walked to the throwing side. He threw the ball. He didn't throw it very hard. It rolled to R.T.'s feet. R.T. picked it up and threw it back to Ernie.

Ernie's tummy flip-flopped. This was it.

"Here it comes," she called. She threw the ball extra hard. It flew across the street. It landed right in front of the McGowans' living room window.

"Hooray!" shouted Michael. "A perfect shot!" He ran to the curb. R.T. and Ernie were right behind him. William was right behind them. Ernie guessed he didn't want to miss anything.

The Martians looked both ways. Then they crossed the street.

Ernie got there first. She bent down to pick up the ball. When she stood up, she was looking right in the McGowans' window. She almost dropped the ball. One of the men inside was looking straight at her. He smiled at her. Then he waved. Ernie waved back weakly.

Then the man got back to work. He climbed a ladder. He hung a blind. It looked as if he was whistling.

The Martians hurried back across the street. They raced up onto Ernie's porch. They flopped down on the floor.

"They are hanging blinds," said Ernie.

"We saw," said R.T. and William and Michael.

"What does it mean?" asked R.T.

"It means that the spy bought the McGowans' house," said Michael. "Now he is fixing it to be Spy Headquarters. The blinds have to go in first, so no one will be able to see what is going on in there."

Ernie's tummy flip-flopped three times. A chill went up her back. Was Michael right? Had she just waved at a spy?

CHAPTER 4

Michael's Close Call

Saturday morning was chore time. Ernie took out the garbage. Then she hurried to the living room window. She looked across the street. Nothing was happening at the McGowans' house yet.

Ernie changed the sheets on her bed. Then she ran back to the window. Still nothing.

She straightened up half of her room. She ran to the window again. Nothing was going on.

She straightened up the other half of her room. Then she went back to the window. Whew! Everything across the street was quiet. She had not missed a thing.

Ernie ate her peanut butter-and-marshmallow sandwich on the porch. She paid close attention to the McGowans' house, but nothing at all was happening. At last, Michael and William and R.T. showed up.

"Any action?" Michael asked.

"Nothing," Ernie told him, "and more nothing."

Michael and R.T. took over the lookout then.

Suddenly, R.T. called out, "Here it comes!"

Ernie looked up the street. There was the strange black car. It drove into the McGowans' driveway.

This time a woman got out. Her hair was pulled back into a ponytail. She was wearing shorts and a T-shirt. She didn't look much like a spy. Then she turned around. She was also wearing a pair of big, black sunglasses.

"Another one!" Michael whispered.

The woman walked to the front door. She unlocked it and went inside.

"It's a spy ring, all right," said Michael.

"And it's getting bigger all the time!" said

R.T. She pointed across the street. A second delivery truck was just coming to a stop.

Again, two men got out. They were not the same men as yesterday, though. And they did not have a key to the house. They carried three big boxes onto the porch. Then they rang the bell. The woman let them in.

"I wonder what was in those boxes," said Michael. "Maybe we'd better play miss-the-ball again."

"We don't have to," said William. He grinned. "I already know what was in those boxes."

"Tell us!" said Ernie and Michael and R.T. all together.

"A computer," said William. "We have the same kind. It came in those exact boxes."

"Of course!" said Michael. "Every spy ring needs a computer."

"Shhh," whispered R.T. "They are coming out again."

Sure enough, the deliverymen and the woman were leaving the house. The men got back into their truck. They drove away. The woman locked the door. Then she got into the black car and drove away, too.

"Let's go over there and snoop around," said Michael.

"What if she comes back?" said William.

"We have time," said Michael. "Come on." He started down the porch steps.

Just then, R.T. sucked in her breath.

Ernie looked up the street. *"Stop, Michael!"* she shouted. The black car was coming back.

Michael flew back onto the porch. "Whew!" he gasped. "That was a close call!"

The car stopped in the driveway. The woman got out. She opened the garage door. She went inside. She came back out with a ladder. She set it up right there in the driveway.

Then she went back to the car. She opened the trunk. She took out a basketball net and a toolbox.

"A basketball net!" said R.T. "Why do spies need a basketball net?"

"Shhh," said Michael. "She will hear you."

The woman fastened the basketball net above the garage door. Then she folded up the ladder. She put it back in the garage. She put the toolbox in the garage, too. Then she shut the garage door, got back into the car, and drove away.

"Weird!" said William.

"I still don't get it," said R.T.

"Me, neither," said Ernie. "Why does a spy need a basketball net?"

"To keep in shape, of course," said Michael. "Spies need to be fast. They need a lot of exercise."

"I don't think so," said William. "Spies don't hang around in their driveways shooting baskets. Just regular people do that. That is why she hung the net. To make Spy Headquarters *look* like a regular house."

"Good thinking, William," said Michael.

William grinned. "I had brain food for breakfast this morning," he said.

R.T. shivered. "I love mysteries!" she said.

Ernie didn't say anything. All she had was questions.

CHAPTER 5

The Spy Code

"The coast is clear," said Michael. "She won't come back. Not twice in one day. Let's go over there."

"Maybe we will find another message," said R.T.

Ernie hoped so. She needed another clue.

The Martians marched across the street. There was no use peeking in windows today. All the new blinds were pulled shut. Maybe the Martians would find a clue in the yard, though.

Ernie and William walked around the house one way. Michael and R.T. walked around the other way. They met in the backyard.

"Find anything?" R.T. asked.

Ernie shook her head. "Just flowers and bushes and a couple of stones," she said. "Did you?"

"Nope," said Michael. He looked very disappointed.

The Martians finished their trips around the house. They met again by the garage. No one had found a thing.

"Sure is a neat yard," said R.T. "The McGowans must have cleaned it up before they moved."

Michael looked through a garage window. There were no blinds there. There was nothing to see, either. "Just the ladder and the toolbox," he told them. He kicked a stone.

Ernie watched the stone bounce down the driveway. It didn't go far, but where it landed made her tummy start flip-flopping again. It landed right next to a postcard. The woman must have dropped it!

Ernie ran down the driveway. She bent down and picked up the postcard. There was a picture of Garfield on the front. She

turned it over. Her tummy dropped to her shoes. She had found what she was looking for, all right. Another clue! Another message, and it was written in code!

"What's that?" asked Michael. "A postcard?"

"What does it say?" asked R.T.

"Is it written in code?" asked William.

Ernie nodded. "I think we had better go home," she told them.

The Martians raced back to Ernie's porch. They sat down in a circle on the floor. Ernie set the postcard in the middle.

"Holy cow!" breathed R.T. She was chewing on her braid again.

"Wow!" said Michael.

"Who is 131513?" asked William.

"Where is the decoder?" asked Ernie.

"Right here," said Michael. He pulled the decoder out of his pocket. It was more wrinkled than yesterday, but they could still read it.

1 = DR   6 = KI
2 = LL   7 = LR
3 = BA   8 = NG
4 = FA   9 = MAB
5 = EA

"Wait a minute," said Ernie. She ran inside for a pad and a pencil.

Ernie drew a postcard on the pad. "Now decode the message," she said. "I'll write it down."

"Three is BA," Michael began. "One is DR. . . ."

When he had finished, Ernie's postcard looked even weirder than the real one.

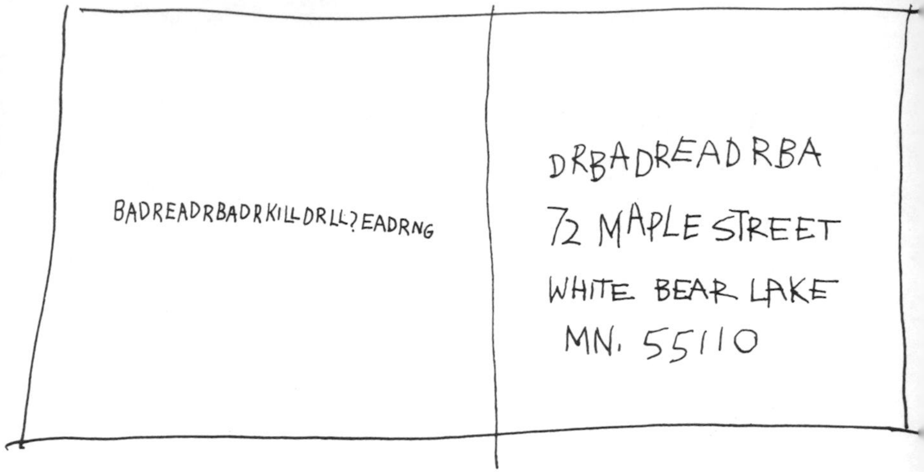

BADREADRBADRKILLDRLL?EADRNG

DRBADREADRBA
72 MAPLE STREET
WHITE BEAR LAKE
MN. 55110

The question mark stood for the 0 in the message. Their decoder didn't say what 0 meant.

"It doesn't make any sense," said Michael.

"Maybe it skips some letters," said R.T.

"Maybe it has extra letters," said William. "Look at this." He picked up Ernie's pad and pencil and circled some of the letters.

BADREADRBADRKILLDRLL?EADRNG

DRBADREADRBA
72 MAPLE STREET
WHITE BEAR LAKE
MN. 55110

"Wow!" said R.T.

"The spy's code name must be Bad Read," said Michael. "This card was sent to Bad Read. And look—the message is written to Bad Read. Those are the first two words."

"I wonder why there is another Bad after Bad Read," said Ernie.

"Why not?" said William. He shivered. "Look at the next word."

Ernie and Michael and R.T. stared at the fourth word. R.T. chewed on her braid. Michael's mouth dropped open. Ernie's tummy flip-flopped.

The fourth word was Kill!

CHAPTER 6

Through the Basement Window

Ernie didn't sleep very well on Saturday night. She tossed. She turned. Every time she shut her eyes, she saw that postcard. Were spies really moving into the McGowans' house? Were they going to kill someone? It did not look good.

Finally, Ernie turned on her light. It was impossible to think in the dark. The dark was too scary.

Ernie slipped out of bed. The postcard was in her treasure box. The treasure box was on her desk. Ernie lifted the lid. She took out the postcard. She climbed back into bed. She looked at the postcard.

The Martians had passed the card back and forth all afternoon. The message had been written in pencil. The writing on it was smudged now, and so was the drawing. Ernie had forgotten all about that drawing. It looked like a finger with a string tied around it. People tied strings around their fingers to help them remember things. What was Bad Read supposed to remember? Remember to kill someone?

Ernie stared at the postcard. She wished she knew where it came from. Spy postcards ought to come from Washington, D.C., Ernie thought. She studied the postmark on this card. Not all of it was there. Some of it was off the top. What was there was *not* Washington, D.C., though. It was COL   , WY.

Ernie put the postcard back in her treasure box. She got back into bed. These spies were not so smart. They wrote important messages in pencil. They lost their messages. Their cards did not come from Washington, D.C. Maybe these spies were not spies after all. Ernie turned out her light. She could go to sleep now.

Sunday was a very quiet day. Michael was visiting his grandma. R.T. was having Family Day. Ernie didn't know where William was, but he did not come over. It was raining again, anyway. It was not a good day for Martian spy work.

Ernie helped Daddy fix a leaky pipe. Then she and Mommy and Daddy played Parcheesi on the living room rug. Then they watched a movie Mommy had rented.

Ernie looked out the window several

times, but nothing was happening across the street. The McGowans' house was still and silent. Ernie guessed that even spies got sick of rain. If they *were* spies, that is.

Monday morning was bright and sunny.

"Why does it always rain on weekends?" Daddy asked at breakfast. "Then on Monday when I have to go to work, it gets nice again."

"It rained all week last week," Ernie reminded him.

Daddy grinned. "Right you are, Ernie," he said. "I guess I should not complain."

The Martians got to Ernie's early, but not quite early enough. Another truck had already arrived. The woman in the black car was there, too. She let the deliverymen in through the McGowans' back door.

"What is it this time?" William whispered.

"Those boxes were awful big," said R.T.

"The truck says Raymond's Woodworks," said Ernie. "What's 'woodworks'?"

"Let's go find out," said Michael.

"No way!" said William. "They are *in* there."

"C'mon, William," said Michael. "This is Maple Street, and we are just kids. They won't hurt us."

"Besides, William," said Ernie. "They may not even be spies."

"*Not spies*?" said Michael. "Of course they are spies."

"I don't know, Michael," Ernie said. "They lose their messages. They write them in pencil. If they are spies, they are not very good ones."

"But what about the code?" said R.T. "Regular grown-ups do not write in code."

"I haven't figured that part out yet," Ernie said.

"Well, I have," said Michael. "They *are* spies. You are wrong this time, Ernie. Now, come on."

He led the way across the street. He tip-toed across the lawn. Ernie and R.T. and William followed him.

Suddenly, Ernie stopped. She had heard something. It sounded like hammering.

Michael had heard it, too. "It's coming from the basement," he whispered. He dropped down onto his knees. He peered through a basement window. "Holy cow," he whispered. "They are building a torture chamber down there. Let's get out of here!" He jumped to his feet and tore across the lawn.

Ernie wanted to see for herself. She knelt down by the window. She peeked inside.

They were building something, all right. There was a counter along one wall. One man was fitting shelves onto the wall above it. There was another counter in the middle of the floor. The other man was attaching a big round saw to it.

"To saw the bodies up," whispered R.T. She grabbed William's hand and raced after Michael.

Ernie got to her feet and followed them, but she did not run. That was no torture

chamber in the McGowans' basement. It was just a workshop. Daddy had one like it in their basement. Mommy gave it to him last Christmas. Ernie had watched the delivery-men set it up. It even had a round saw.

"Hurry up, Ernie!" shouted William. He was jumping up and down on the other side of the street. "They are coming!"

Ernie looked over her shoulder.

The two men were leaving the house now. The woman was standing on the back porch. She was talking with the men. They did not notice Ernie.

Ernie looked both ways. Then she crossed the street. She joined the Martians on her front porch.

"You have to be more careful, Ernie!" said William. "They could have got you then!"

Ernie smiled. "I don't think so, William." Then she said to the Martians, "Meet me back here after lunch." She opened her front door and went inside.

CHAPTER 7

The Spy Postcard

Ernie went straight to her bedroom and shut the door. It was time to think. Her bedroom was a very good place for thinking. Everything she needed was there. Ellie and Teddy and Dina sat on her bed to keep her company. The shell wind chimes that she had made herself hung by the open window. Their cheery clatter kept her happy. All her important books were in her bookcase. A map of the United States hung over her desk. Her treasure box, with the postcard inside it, was on her desk. Paper and pencils were in the top drawer.

Ernie pulled out a pad of paper and a pencil. Writing things down always helped. First she made a list of all the deliveries.

window blinds
computer
basketball net
workshop

It could all be spy stuff, Ernie guessed. Spies would need window blinds. They would need a computer, too. They could need a workshop. The only problem was that basketball net. What spy needed a basketball net?

Ernie felt surer and surer that this wasn't spy stuff at all. It was *family* stuff. Families needed to cover their windows, too. And they needed computers. And they needed workshops. And, most important, families often needed basketball nets.

The trouble was the code. Ernie opened her treasure box. She took out the postcard. R.T. was right about one thing: Regular grown-ups did not write messages in codes.

Ernie studied the card. It was printed in pencil. She thought about that. When Mommy sent a card, she did not print it. She wrote it with all the letters tied together. She did not write it in pencil, either. She wrote it in ink. She did not need to erase as much as Ernie did.

Ernie looked closely at this printing. Sure enough, there were places where it had been erased. Whoever printed this had made some mistakes.

Ernie looked more closely at the printing. It wasn't neat like Daddy's printing. It didn't march in straight lines. The letters were not all the same size.

"Boing!" shouted Ernie. Suddenly, she had it. This postcard was not written by any spy. This postcard was written the way *she* would write it. This postcard was written by a kid! Kids wrote in code all the time. All she had to do now was decode this kid's code. She did

not need the spy decoder for that. All she needed was her eagle eye.

Ernie heard the telephone ring. She heard Mommy answer it. Then she heard a knock on her door. "Come in," she said.

Mommy opened the door. "That was William's mother," she said. "William's parents are going out tonight. William is going to stay with us."

"Great!" said Ernie. A plan was forming in Ernie's mind. Maybe William could help her crack this case.

The Martians were back right after lunch. So was the mystery woman in the black car. And she had something else with her: a dollhouse. She carried it inside. Then she drove away again.

"A dollhouse?" said William.

"It's a model," Michael explained. "A model of the place they are spying on. Remember that postcard? They are going to *kill* someone in that house."

"And saw him up in their torture chamber," said R.T.

"And bury him in the backyard," said Michael.

Ernie did not say anything yet. That lady was no spy, Ernie was almost sure of it. But she still needed proof. She needed to decode that code, and she planned to do it tonight!

CHAPTER 8

Decoding the Code

Mommy made spaghetti for supper. Spaghetti was William's favorite food. Ernie hoped it was his brain food, too.

After supper, Ernie took William to her room. She shut the door. She got the postcard from her treasure box. She pulled the list of deliveries out of her desk drawer. She wrote down one more thing: dollhouse.

Ernie put two pillows on the floor. She and William plopped down on them. Then she handed him the list. "Look at this, William," she said.

window blinds
computer
basketball net
workshop
dollhouse

"It's a list of all the spy stuff," said William.

Ernie shook her head. "This is not *spy* stuff, William. This is *family* stuff. We have all of these things right here in this house—except for the basketball net."

William scratched his head. Then he began to smile. "And we have all of it at my house, too—except for the dollhouse." Then his smile disappeared. "But what about the postcard, Ernie? Families do not write in code."

"I think someone in this family does," said Ernie. She handed William the card. Then she explained everything she had figured out about it. She made a new list. It was about the postcard.

1. This card did not come from Washington, D.C.

2. This card is printed.
3. It is printed in pencil.
4. Some letters were erased.
5. The lines are not straight.
6. The letters are not neat.
7. A KID WROTE THIS CARD!!!!

William jumped to his feet. He was getting excited now. "I think you are right, Ernie!" he said. "Look at this." He turned the card over. "Spies do not send Garfield postcards."

"They do not keep losing their messages, either," said Ernie.

"But what about the code, Ernie? And the drawing?" asked William. "What do they mean?"

"That is what we are going to figure out," said Ernie. "We are going to crack this code tonight! What do you know about codes, William?"

"I make them sometimes," said William.

Now Ernie jumped to her feet. "How?" she asked. "How do you make your codes, William? Show me."

William sat down again. "I draw pictures for all the letters," he said. "Like this." He began to draw. Ernie watched over his shoulder.

A   B   C   D   E   F   G

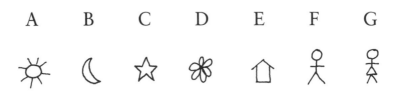

"Wow!" said Ernie. "You mean you draw a picture for every letter in the alphabet?" William nodded. "That is a lot of pictures!" said Ernie.

William grinned. "I am a good draw-er, Ernie," he reminded her.

"You sure are." Ernie sighed. "I could never do that. I would have to make a simpler code."

She stared at the postcard. *Boing!* There it was! The simpler code was right in front of her. It was a number code!

Ernie grabbed the pad from William. "Look at this." She began to write.

A	B	C	D	E	F	G	H	I	J	K	L	M
1	2	3	4	5	6	7	8	9	10	11	12	13

N	O	P	Q	R	S	T	U	V	W	X	Y	Z
14	15	16	17	18	19	20	21	22	23	24	25	26

"Now read me the numbers on that post-card," she said. As William read, Ernie decoded the name above the address.

"One," read William. Ernie wrote A. "Three," read William. Ernie wrote C. "One," read William. Ernie wrote A. "Five," read William. Ernie wrote E. "One again," said William. Ernie wrote A. "Three again," said William. Ernie wrote C.

Then William stopped reading.

"Is that all?" asked Ernie.

William nodded. "Let me see the message."

Ernie showed him what she had written: ACAEAC.

"That doesn't make any sense at all, Ernie," said William.

"It sure doesn't." Ernie agreed. She stared at the postcard. Then she stared at her new decoder. Was she doing something wrong? 1 was A, all right. And 3 was C. She looked at the rest of the alphabet.

"Wait a minute," she said. "One and three are also thirteen! And thirteen is M. What's next, William?"

"One, then five," said William.

"Fifteen," said Ernie. "That's O!"

"Then one and three again," said William.

"M again!" said Ernie. "MOM—Mom! This kid was writing to his mom. We did it, William. We cracked the code."

"Quick!" said William. "Let's do the other side."

When they had finished, they finally had a message that made sense.

3   1   5   1   3   1   6   2   1   2   0   5   1   8
C   O   M   P   U   T   E   R

"Hooray!" shouted Ernie. She began to dance around the room.

"We did it!" shouted William. He was hopping up and down. "Now it all makes sense. Even the drawing!"

Ernie stopped dancing. "I keep forgetting about that drawing," she said. "What does it mean, William? You are the good draw-er."

William grinned. "It's simple," he said. "This drawing is of a string tied around a finger. This kid wants his mom to remember something. He wants her to remember a computer."

"And she *did* remember it!" Ernie shouted. She jumped onto her bed. She felt so happy, she just had to bounce. "His mom remembered to get him a computer."

"There is just one question left," said William.

Ernie stopped bouncing. "What question?" she asked.

"Who was that man we saw on the first day?" said William. "And why didn't he have a key?"

CHAPTER 9

The Spy Lady

Ernie woke up with the birds on Thursday. This was the day to solve the case of the Maple Street spies. This was the day she would find out who the man without a key was. Ernie was not quite sure how she would do it. She was just sure that she would.

Ernie was not the only one who was up early. The telephone was already ringing.

Mommy answered it. "It's for you, lamb," she told Ernie. "It's William."

Ernie picked up the phone. "Hi, William," she said.

"Is she there yet?" William asked.

"Who?" asked Ernie.

"The spy lady, of course," said William.

Ernie giggled. "She is not a spy lady, William. And of course she is not there yet. It is too early."

"I know she is not a spy, Ernie. But we don't know her name yet. I have to call her something." William paused. "Go look out your window just in case. Okay?"

"Okay," said Ernie. She lay down the phone and walked to the living room. Her tummy flip-flopped. The not-a-spy lady *was* there. She was just getting out of her car.

Ernie ran back to the telephone. "She *is* there!" she told William. "How did you know?"

"I didn't," said William. "I just hoped. I'm coming over right now."

William's phone slammed down in Ernie's ear. He was moving fast. She had better eat her breakfast in a hurry.

Ernie and William stood on the porch. The not-a-spy lady was in the McGowans' front yard. She was planting flowers.

"That makes it for sure," said Ernie. "Spies do not plant flowers. I am sure of it."

"Right," said William, "but people being spied *on* plant flowers."

"Huh?" said Ernie. "William, what are you talking about?"

"Listen, Ernie," William whispered. "I thought about this all last night. That man last week—the one we saw first—he looked just like a spy. He didn't have a key. He even wore sunglasses in the rain. Maybe he was spying on *her*."

"We had better warn her," said Ernie. "Come on, William."

Ernie and William crossed the street. The not-a-spy lady looked up. She held a spade in one hand. She held a pansy in the other. She looked surprised.

"Well, good morning, early birds," she said. "Who do I have the pleasure of meeting this morning?"

The not-a-spy lady talked funny, but she seemed nice. She was smiling, anyway.

"I'm Ernie," said Ernie.

"And I'm William," said William. "We have come to warn you."

A lock of hair hung over the not-a-spy lady's eye. She brushed it away with the back of her spade hand. "Warn me of what?" she asked. She looked surprised.

"I live across the street from you," Ernie explained. "My friends and I have been watching your house all week."

"We think we saw a spy here last Thursday," William added.

The not-a-spy lady laughed. She set down her spade and her pansy. She took off her gardening gloves. She looked closely at William. Then she looked closely at Ernie. She stopped laughing, but her eyes twinkled.

"I think this calls for a serious discussion," she said. "How about some milk and cookies to go with it?"

Ernie and William nodded. The lady went inside. She came back out with three glasses of milk and a plate of chocolate chip-raisin cookies.

"I always put in raisins," she said. "My

daughter thinks raisins are brain food."

Ernie nodded. "They are," she said. "Bananas, too."

Then the three of them sat down on the not-a-spy lady's porch. Ernie and William took turns explaining all about the man in the raincoat and sunglasses. When they had finished, the not-a-spy lady passed them the cookie plate again.

"Have another cookie," she said. Then she told them all about the spy man. When she finished, Ernie and William were both laughing.

"We sure got fooled this time," said Ernie.

"Especially Michael," said William. "He is never going to believe this. He really wants you to be a spy, I think," he told the lady.

"He has to believe it," said Ernie. "We have proof. But he sure will be surprised."

William began to giggle. "We could surprise him even more," he said.

"What do you mean?" asked Ernie.

"Listen," said William, and he told Ernie and the not-a-spy lady his plan.

CHAPTER 10

William's Plan

It wasn't easy to make the plan work. The not-a-spy lady had to get ready. And Ernie and William had to delay Michael and R.T. until she was.

They did it, though. Ernie found Michael in the Martian clubhouse. William caught R.T. at the corner. He brought her to the clubhouse, too.

"What is going on?" asked Michael.

"Why did you bring us here?" asked R.T. "We should be on Ernie's porch, spying on the spy house."

"That is exactly where we are going," said William. "Come on. It's time now." He practically dragged R.T. out the clubhouse door.

Ernie pulled on Michael's arm.

"Cut that out," said Michael. "We were coming over, anyway. You don't have to pull us."

"Oh, yes, we do!" said Ernie. "You are in for a *big* surprise. We don't want you to miss it."

By then they had reached Ernie's corner. Suddenly, Michael stopped short. His mouth dropped open.

R.T. stopped, too. "Look who is on your porch, Ernie!" she gasped.

"It's the spy!" said Michael.

There, on Ernie's front porch, sat the first spy—the man in the raincoat. He was still wearing sunglasses. His hat was pulled right down to them.

William coughed. He sounded scared, but Ernie knew better. Ernie knew he was just trying hard not to laugh. She was trying, too.

Ernie tugged on Michael's arm. "Come on," she told him.

Michael thought for a second. Then he

stomped his foot. "No old spy can scare a Martian!" he said. "Right, R.T.?"

"Right, Michael!" R.T. agreed, and the four Martians marched onto Ernie's porch.

"Good morning," said the not-a-spy lady in a very low voice. In her outfit, she looked just like a man. Now she sounded like a man, too.

Then in her regular voice, she said, "I'm very happy to meet you." She pulled off her hat. Her hair fell to her shoulders. "I'm always happy to meet Martians." She took off her sunglasses.

R.T.'s mouth fell open. One of her braids fell out of it. Michael sucked in his breath.

William clapped his hands. He jumped up and down. "This lady was the spy man, Michael!" he shouted. "She was the spy lady, too. But she was never a spy at all. She is just a regular person who is moving into the McGowans' house." William paused for breath. "Regular except for her cookies," he added. "She makes brain-food cookies. They are super-duper."

"Her name is Mrs. Cridland," Ernie added. "She is getting the McGowans' house ready for her family. They are moving here from Colter Bay, Wyoming. That's who the computer and the basketball net and the workshop and the dollhouse were for, Michael."

The not-a-spy lady reached out to shake hands with Michael. Michael put his hands behind his back.

"Then how come you wore sunglasses?" Michael asked. "Only spies wear sunglasses in the rain."

"Only spies and people with an eye infection," said Mrs. Cridland. "I was just getting over it."

But Michael still wouldn't shake hands. "Then how come you didn't have a key?" he asked.

Mrs. Cridland laughed. "You certainly are suspicious, Michael," she said. "I didn't have a key because the man who was supposed to meet me with it didn't show up. I had to go to his office to get it."

"Well," said Michael, "I guess that explains it, all right." He held out his hand. "How old are your kids?"

"Wait a minute!" said R.T. "It isn't all explained yet. What about the postcard code?"

"Yeah," said Michael. He pulled back his hand. "What about the postcard code?"

"Oh, Michael," said Ernie. "That postcard was from one of Mrs. Cridland's kids. He was reminding her to get him a computer. Look." She showed Michael and R.T. how she and William had decoded the postcard.

"I promised him he could have one when we moved," said Mrs. Cridland.

"But what about this?" asked Michael. He pulled the decoder from his pocket.

1 = DR   6 = KI

2 = LL   7 = LR

3 = BA   8 = NG

4 = FA   9 = MAB

5 = EA

Ernie and William and Mrs. Cridland all laughed.

"That is the best thing of all," said Ernie.

"And Ernie knew what it was all along," said William. "Initials!"

"Whose initials?" asked R.T.

"Most of them are initials of *rooms*!" Ernie explained.

"Rooms?" said R.T. and Michael in the same breath.

"Yup," said Mrs. Cridland. "They are my codes for the moving boxes. The things in the number one boxes go to the dining room. Number three boxes go to the bathroom. Number fours go to the family room. Number sixes to the kitchen. Number sevens to the living room. Number nines to the master bedroom."

"But what about the twos and fives and eights?" said R.T. "Where are LL and EA and NG?"

"You mean *who* are LL and EA and NG," said Ernie. "Those are Mrs. Cridland's kids. Louisa Lynn and Edward Albert and Nancy

Grace. Boxes marked with twos and fives and eights go to their rooms."

"Neat-o!" said R.T.

"Are any of these kids my age?" Michael asked.

Mrs. Cridland nodded. "Two of them," she said. "Edward Albert and Nancy Grace are twins. They will get here tomorrow."

"I guess it's okay, then," said Michael. He held out his hand. Mrs. Cridland shook it. Michael grinned. "But it sure was nice having spies on Maple Street for a little while."

Mrs. Cridland held out a paper bag. There were chocolate chip-brain food cookies inside it. "Have a cookie, Michael," she said. "Who knows? Maybe you'll uncover another spy ring next week."

"Yeah," said Michael. "Some spies from space would be good."

Ernie looked at William. William looked at R.T. R.T. looked at Ernie. Then all together they looked at Michael. "No more spies on Maple Street!" they shouted. Then they each had another brain-food cookie.